Stories of the Dead

Kori Elias

Published by Trellis Publishing, 2021.

STORIES OF THE DEAD

First edition. July 5, 2021.

ISBN: 979-8224070947

Written by Kori Elias.

STORIES OF THE DEAD

KORI ELIAS

Tremors

Chapter One

The house was dark when she got back from court. Not that she had expected any differently. It was the middle of December, after all, and now that she lived here alone...well, she'd have been significantly more freaked out if even the porch light had been on. Marie's hands shook as she pulled her keys out of her purse and the key tremored as she entered it into the lock, turning it and wincing at the thunderous creak as she pushed the door open.

Her head had been pounding since noon, nearly five hours ago now. She had forgone her usual morning painkiller in favor of keeping a clear head, only to find the task next to impossible. Every word her lawyer had uttered sounded like nails on a chalkboard and the judge's had been worse. Even Jeremy's voice, which had once soothed her through panic attacks and serenaded her into a puddle, only served to hammer the nails in at the base of her skull. By the time court was adjourned for the day, Marie's fingernails had made sharp little crescents in the heels of her hands that had not yet lost their sting.

Taking a deep breath, she walked silently through the house, willing her legs to keep moving through the pain as she made her way up the stairs and down the hall to the bathroom. She didn't even bother to turn on the light as she reached into the medicine cabinet for the familiar little bottle of pills; oxycontin. It had been refilled far more times than necessary, despite the doctor's wishes, and then more after he'd refused to prescribe it for her. She'd taken to buying it from a neighbor kid down the street who sold them to pay for his college education; she often joked with him about how he should remember to thank her in his valedictorian speech for how much money she had funneled to him behind her husband's back.

Ex-husband, her mind supplied as Jeremy's appeared. They were about to get a divorce. Ten years of marriage—of love and late nights spent dancing and watching movies cuddling on the couch; of dancing to no music at all and bickering over what they would have for dinner; of arguing over where they would spend the holidays and what they would name the children they never even had—was all about to come crashing down. That's why she needed these pills, she told herself. That's why they were completely necessary. It wasn't about the injury she'd sustained last winter when she slipped in the icy driveway and hurt her back; it was about the way her heart ached whenever he was around. The way the very sight of him reminded her of things she would never be able to have with him around.

Marie poured two pills into her hand and—not for the first time—imagined what would happen if she downed the remainder of the bottle. Would her heart stop beating instantly or would she fall asleep and her breathing stop slowly as she lay on the bathroom floor, curled up next to the sink? She'd thought many times about doing it in the last year since her accident had left her bedridden for close to ten weeks, her spine leaving her temporarily paralyzed while also sending pinpricks of pain up and down her back. The doctor had prescribed her oxy, intent on having her wean off of it over time, but she hadn't been able to—especially after Jeremy had made his "decision".

Just the thought of it filled Marie with anger and she plucked another pill from the bottle and reached for a glass. The pills fell easily down her throat with a single sip of water and Marie breathed a deep sigh of relief as she made her way back up the hall to the master bedroom. The bed was blissfully empty as she dropped her body heavily down on it and climbed under the covers, fully clothed. Closing her eyes, she allowed the oxy to drag her down into the depths of a dreamless sleep.

Chapter Two

When Marie's eyes opened, her mouth felt as dry as the Sahara and her back ached. There was also a familiar pressure in her bladder and she pushed herself into a sitting position, groaning as her muscles protested the movement. Removing her clothes piece by piece, Marie stood and made her way to the attached bathroom, ignoring the chill that moved from her bare feet, all the way to the top of her spine.

Her eyes were barely open as she went through the motions; relieving herself, washing her face, brushing her teeth, and popping a couple more pills to get rid of the headache that was already starting to creep up the back of her skull. When she returned to her bedroom, she flopped blindly back down onto the bed and shrouded herself in the warmth of her 1,000-count Egyptian cotton sheets. She took a deep breath and allowed her body to relax, feeling the oxy start to pump through her veins and take all the pain away.

"Stop hogging the sheets, Mar," a deep, groggy voice said in her ear and Marie nearly launched herself from the mattress, turning with wide, horrified eyes at the man on the other side of the bed, her breath frozen in her lungs.

"Jeremy?" she huffed, narrowing her eyes at him. Her head felt light and her body was numb, but she could still feel anger coursing through her. "What the hell are you doing here?"

"Uh...sleeping?" he grunted in reply, turning over onto his back. Marie was taken aback by how youthful his face looked. The beard he'd begun sporting over the last several months was gone now, as were the bags that usually sat just under his eyes. He furrowed his brows at her, his eyes squinted in confusion, his mouth twisted to one side. "Are you okay, babe? You don't look so good."

"What...why...why are you here?" Marie stuttered, feeling her legs begin to shake underneath her. "We're...you...why?"

"Babe, you're slurring," Jeremy said, his voice filled with concern, his hand reaching out for her as he sat up. "Sit down before you fall and hurt yourself." Marie did as she was told, but only because she couldn't bear to hold herself up any longer. She fell to the bed with a sigh, her mouth still gaping open as she stared at her ex, who was giving her a look that she almost didn't recognize. Jeremy's dark brown eyes shone with concern and his large hand reached out to stroke her cheek, the pads of his fingers softer than they've been in the last decade.

Marie laid her smaller hand over his and closed her eyes, breathing him in, allowing his once-familiar scent to envelop her, the heat of his skin against hers warm her body, and the soft stroke of his thumb to lull her into a sense of contentment that no amount of pills has ever been able to give her. Surely she was just having a drug-induced dream and the second her eyes opened, he would be gone and she would find herself lying on her side in bed, alone. She might as well soak it all up while she could, right?

Marie counted to ten in her head, as slowly as possible, telling herself that once she reached the last number, she would open her eyes and be done with this hallucination. It took nearly a full minute to do this and another to work up the courage to finally allow her lids to lift up until...

But when her eyes opened, her husband was still sitting in front of her, that concerned look still etched on his beautiful face. Marie screamed.

Chapter Three

Marie sat, prone, in the corner of her bedroom, her knees pulled up to her chest, body shaking and aching all over, her head pounding, mouth dry, and eyes wide with fear. This could not be happening. Her husband—or rather, a younger version of her husband—could not be standing there, looking at her like she was insane, his brown hair ruffled and much thicker than it had been as of late. Marie remembered running her hands through it, remembered brushing her fingers over his chin, her fingers tingling with the scruff at his jaw. She loved that scruff.

Or, at least, she *used* to love that scruff. Lately, it had been annoyance for both of them. Jeremy had taken to letting it grow for a week at a time and then shaving it all off when it became too itchy for him to bare. It no longer looked ruggedly handsome on him. Instead it made him look like a homeless person, and Marie had told him that more than once. Perhaps that was why he'd decided to stay at the office so many late nights. Maybe she had been the one to push him into the arms of that slut he'd divorced her for.

The thought incensed Marie to the point that she found herself giving this younger version of Jeremy a deathly glare, which only served to confuse him further.

"Mar?" he said. "Are you okay? Seriously, you look terrible right now. What the hell happened?"

"*You* happened," Marie growled at him, the sound ripping from her throat. It hurt just to speak, but the anger threatened to burst forth from her lips, her fists clenching at her knees. "You did *all of this*."

"Wha—how?" Marie pressed her lips together, still glaring at him. Jeremy stepped forward and she pressed herself against the wall. He got the hint, his movement halting. "What did I do? Why are you so angry at me? Why are you being like this?" He motioned to her prone body, in the corner, pressing herself further against the wall.

"You should know what you did," Marie snapped. "It happened less than a year ago!"

"Obviously, I don't," Jeremy sighed. "Could you please just tell me?"

Marie pressed her lips into a think line again, then sighed, rolling her eyes. Her body didn't relax any further, her muscles still taught, her joints still locked up in this position. Still, she forced herself to meet his eyes, to look up into the face of the man who'd ruined her life, though he had absolutely no idea how.

"I was pregnant," she said, at last, and Jeremy's eyes widened.

"Y-you were?" he gasped. "When? We've only been together a little over a year! How—when? Why wouldn't you tell me?"

"I *did* tell you," Marie said, losing patience and feeling the pain in her back double. She had to stand, had to get to her medication. "You were thrilled."

"I was?" Marie nodded. "Then what happened? Where's the baby?"

Marie felt the dread and sadness start to well up in her, causing the all-too-familiar ache in her heart. Her hands shook and the need inside her grew—to escape, to have her pills, to be okay again. But she wouldn't be, she knew. She would never be okay again. She opened her mouth, the words dry on her tongue.

"She died."

Chapter Four

Marie remembered her last day without pain like it was yesterday.

It was the middle of December, early morning. She had told Jeremy just last month that they were expecting their first child. At their most recent sonogram, they learned that they would have a daughter—a little girl who would, without a doubt, be just as stubborn as her mother and have a smile as charming as her father's. They were overjoyed with the news and Jeremy had made plans to start painting the nursery as soon as possible. He already had swatches of pinks and purples and light blues on their bedside table, which they'd gone over the night before, making plans together.

A baby was just the thing they needed, Marie thought, to complete their family. They'd wanted children for the last decade, but they hadn't really had the time, between their careers and so many other factors, to really plan on having a baby. Things had finally started to slow down and they were in a good place now. It seemed like the perfect time.

Marie got up that morning, pulling herself out of bed, her hand pressed protectively to the slight swell on her belly, and stretched out her body before making her way to the bathroom, her ankles already swelling with the pregnancy, her back aching just slightly. She went through all of the usual steps to start her morning, leaving her husband in bed to sleep a little longer.

By the time she was dressed, he was just starting to stir, smiling sleepily up at her, and the slight darkness of his jaw beckoning to her lips. Marie had leaned down to kiss him, reverently, giggling when he tried to pull her down onto the bed with him. She slapped his hands away from her hips and backed away from the bed, shaking her head. He had pouted adorably up at her and she rolled her eyes as she slipped into a pair of heels, reveling the fact that her feet hadn't swelled too much to wear her usual work shoes.

"Did you ice the driveway last night?" she asked, grabbing her coat from the closet.

"I'm pretty sure I did," Jeremy replied, turning back over in bed, reaching for her pillow to drag against his chest. "Still, be careful out there. It's supposed to be a cold one, today."

"Of course," Marie said as she exited the bedroom, sparing him one last glance and blowing him a kiss. "I'll see you later, sweetheart," she'd said.

"Love you," Jeremy called out after her.

"Love you, too!" she'd giggled. Looking back, that may have been the last time she'd ever truly meant those words to him.

Making her way outside, Marie had stepped carefully down the driveway to her car, checking her phone for any emergency emails from her boss as she dug her keys out with her other hand and unlocked and started the car, hoping fruitlessly that it would be warm by the time she sat down at the driver's seat.

It didn't matter if it would have been, however, as in the next second she was on the ground, her body paralyzed with pain, her head pounding, the breath knocked out of her, preventing her from saying anything or even calling for help. All she could do was just lie there for several minutes, until her husband walked out, a trash bag in hand.

"Marie?" he had gasped, dropping the bag and running to her side. "MARIE!" She found herself looking up into his chocolate brown eyes, which were frantic with worry. But all she could think, as the world went black around her, was that there was no salt on the driveway.

Chapter Five

Jeremy was silent for a long while, just staring at her in shock.

"I...I did this?" he asked, motioning to her. "I...but...what happened next? How does that...how?" His ability to form full, coherent sentences had apparently left him.

"I lost the baby," Marie informed him, feeling numb at the vocalization. It had devastated her when the doctor informed them that the baby had not survived the impact of her fall. "They'd had to cut her out of me and ended up damaging something inside. I can get pregnant again, but there's an increased risk of an ectopic pregnancy, or complications." She grit her teeth. "*You* decided that it wasn't worth that risk."

"You mean I..." He looked down at his lap and Marie nodded.

"You got a vasectomy while I was still in the hospital, told me that we could adopt or get a surrogate. You didn't even ask or consider what *I* wanted. You didn't care that I would rather have carried *my own child*."

Jeremy was silent for a moment.

"What did we name her?" he asked, quietly.

"Maura," Marie replied. "It was my grandmother's name; I was named after her, sort of. You thought it would a nice commemoration."

"And what did you think?"

"I was too high to care," Marie said, monotonously.

Jeremy sighed. "What happened to you, Mar?" he asked. "You used to be so full of life and love and...magic. What happened?"

"*YOU HAPPENED*!" Marie screamed, finally pushing herself to her feet, standing a bit unsteadily. "THIS IS ALL YOUR FAULT! YOU DID THIS TO ME! YOU CAUSED EVERYTHING! YOU KILLED MY DAUGHTER!"

Jeremy took a step back, the guilt shining on his face. Marie knew that it wasn't fair to blame all of her pain on him. She knew that it wasn't his fault for, however it happened, he was not the Jeremy that she knew and loathed today. He was the man she had fallen in love with; the man that she had wanted to spend the rest of her life with. It wasn't his fault.

Still, she couldn't help hating him. He had the face of the man who had ruined her life and that was enough for Marie. It was more than enough.

Jeremy, for his part, stood his ground, conviction burning in his eyes as they locked with Marie's. "I'm going to fix it," he promised. "I swear I will. I'll fix this. I will."

Marie looked him in the eye and shook her head. "You can't," she said, her voice gravelly, practically choking on her own sobs. "There's no way."

She said nothing more, turning on her heel and practically sprinting into the bathroom, opening the cupboard and pulling out her oxy. She tore off the cap and poured the remainder of her pills into her palm, then reached for her glass and filled it with water. In an instant, Marie shoved all the pills into her mouth and then down the entirety of the glass of water, choking slightly as some went down the wrong pipe. At the same time, there was a pounding at the bathroom door.

"Mar! Marie, let me in!" Jeremy cried through the door. "Please! We have to talk! Marie!"

Marie didn't answer him. Instead, she climbed into the bathtub and settled onto her back, letting the oxy begin to relax her. Soon, she thought, it would be all over. Soon, she would be at peace. Finally, she would be at peace.

Epilogue

Marie is awoken to loud, insistent cries, muffled but enough to have her jumping out of bed before she even realizes what she's doing. She starts for the door, but then a hand wraps around her wrist and she is pulled back.

"Don't worry, sweetheart," a familiar, tired voice says. "I'll get her." Marie's eyes widen as she turns to see her ex-husband sit up in the bed beside her. There are slight wrinkles on his face, bags under his eyes, and scruff on his jaw. He gives her a tired smile as he stands, in his white t-shirt and boxers, and stretches out his limbs before making his way out the door to where the cries are coming from.

Marie watches him in awe and confusion, taking a single step forward, surprised that, for the first time, there's no ache in her back—at least, not like the debilitating one that used to bring her to her knees—and only a slight weariness in her muscles, as if she's been awake for days.

Still, as tired as she is, Marie finds herself walking out into the hallway and down the hall to the guest room, which is now open. When she gets there, she sees that it's no longer painted plain white, but rather purple. Jeremy sits in a rocking chair with a squirmy little bundle in his arms, chubby hands reaching out towards him as he attempts to feed her a bottle.

Maura, Marie thinks as she steps into the room. There's a crib in one corner and a changing table next to it. The chair that Jeremy is rocking the baby in is surrounded by all kinds of stuffed animals and small baby toys. His smile is wide and loving as he looks down at the baby in his arms, a tuft of blonde hair sticking out from beneath her white cap. Marie takes a step forward and he looks up at her, offering her a loving smile.

"Sweetheart," he says. "It's alright; I told you I'd get her. You need to sleep a little more; you have work in the morning."

Marie is struck dumb by this. It's more consideration that she's seen from him in a long time. It makes her heart skip a beat and it causes a flutter in the bit of her stomach. She steps forward and reaches down to place a kiss on the scruff of his cheek.

"There's no place I'd rather be," she whispers in his ear as she looks down into their daughter's beautiful, deep brown eyes.

THE END

OBSESSION

CASSIE BLAKE

Chapter One

The face that stared back at her was haggard, completely devoid of any and all makeup. There were bags under her eyes from waking up before the sun, tiny wrinkles in the corners of her eyes and around her lips from forcing smiles and laughter at those who were just not that funny. Her nose was covered in freckles that had not seen the light of day since she was a young girl, well before she found herself in a generously-sized dressing room, sitting a vanity with every kind of beauty product she'd wanted as a teenager.

Celeste studied the features she only got to see at this time of the day, marveled in the paleness of her natural lips, the darkness of her skin before it was lightened by camera-ready makeup. Next to her left hand was a pile of fashion magazines, all with her smiling, made up face staring up at her, caramel eyes sparkling in the unseen stage lights, white teeth glowing unnaturally. In the mirror, Celeste could see that one of her top teeth was just slightly crooked; there was no sign of it in any of the magazine spreads she'd done in the last year.

Sometimes, she wondered if her life was all just one big lie. She was positive that nobody would recognize her if she walked out of this room, out of this studio, out of this building without an ounce of mascara or foundation or blush on her face. Without her hair—which naturally fell in springy, golden-brown curls—straightened or a wig laid over it, she would be just another face in the crowd; a chameleon. Sometimes, she wondered if she would prefer to be invisible, rather than have the life she had now, where everybody knew her by name.

Celeste Diaz.

It wasn't even her real name. Well, Diaz was. But Celeste wasn't. Her real name was Maria Celestina Andujar Diaz. It was a mouthful and her very first agent had suggested shortening it to something a little more...attractive. Her mother had initially been insulted by the insinuation that her daughter couldn't be a model with the name she'd been given, but eventually agreed to call her fifteen-year-old Celeste, which sounded more French than Spanish, but at least she was allowed to keep her last name.

It had been nearly fifteen years since that day and now, as Celeste pushed thirty, she felt herself getting tired of the whole charade. Many of the magazines on her vanity had already begun to suggest that she was "too old" to be a model any longer. That she should start thinking about furthering her career; perhaps by acting or singing or doing something else to allow younger, hotter girls to get their chance in front of the camera. They were as unapologetic about this as Celeste was about soaking in the limelight for the moment. As tired as she was about being 'fake', she absolutely loved having her picture taken. This had been true since she was a little girl and it wasn't about to change now.

Still, she wished that she could leave the house looking like herself for once. Not that she really even knew what 'herself' looked like anymore. Was it the woman staring back at her in the mirror? Or was it the dozen or so images of her smiling up from the cover of magazines? She had no idea.

A knock on her door had Celeste turning in her chair and nearly tipping it over as she hastened to stand up. "Yes?" she called out, clearing her throat.

"Sorry to disturb you, Miss Diaz," she heard from the outside. It was one of the stagehands, no doubt. Female; probably Adrienne. "But you have a call. It should have been patched through if you choose to answer."

"A call?" Celeste murmured, walking over to her couch, adjacent to the phone on an end table. The 'call waiting' light was blinking red, right below the time, which read: 6:24. Who would call her this early? Perhaps it was her publicist, George, letting her know that she got another job or that he'd be late. Either of those was just as likely as the other. "I'll take it," Celeste called towards the door.

"Okay, Ma'am," Adrienne said. "Amanda and Carlisle also want you to know that they're on their way and should be here within the half hour to start on hair and makeup."

"Thanks," Celeste said as she reached for the phone, picking it up and then pressing the blinking light until she could hear the click on the other end. "Hello? This is Celeste speaking."

There was silence for a long moment. "This is really you?" the voice on the other end said finally, sounding out of breath and a little tinny.

"Yes," Celeste answered. "And who is this?"

"Celeste," they hissed, dragging out the 'S' in her name like a snake. It sent shivers down her spine. "I'm your biggest fan."

Her heart dropped. How had they gotten through to this line? Her contract specifically said no fan calls. Only business. "Who are you?" she asked again, desperately trying to keep her voice even.

"I'm the person who's going to kill you," the voice croaked into the phone. Then the line went dead.

Chapter Two

"Miss Diaz, it's a real pleasure to meet you. I'm such a big fan."

Celeste was struck dumb by the man's words, her eyes widening slightly as she turned to look at George, who'd shown up just as she hung up with the police. Her furrowed brows asked a silent question that she could not yet voice. *Is he serious?*

The man who was currently fangirling over her was Officer Andrew Miller, a skinny white man with a shiny bald head and big brown eyes. He mooned over her, not even bothering to reach for the notepad clearly visible in his chest pocket. This was who the emergency dispatcher had sent over? George just shrugged and shook his head, the colored lenses of his round John Lennon glasses falling down his nose with the movement.

Celeste took a deep breath and offered Officer Miller a kind smile. "Always nice to meet a fan," she said. "Now, if we could get back to the matter at hand..."

"Oh, yes, of course," the officer said, finally reaching for his notepad and clearing his throat. "The dispatcher told us that you were, um, contacted by somebody who threatened to, um, kill you?"

"Yes," Celeste said, tightening her hold on the robe wrapped around her body, the thick cotton soothing to the touch. "He—they said that they were going to kill me. And that they're also my biggest fan."

"Oh, but you must get that all the time," Officer Miller chuckled. "I mean, you're a beautiful, very famous woman, right?"

"Yes, but we typically filter out those calls," George cut in, his gruff voice making him sound twice as angry as he looked. "No fans are supposed to be able to directly contact Celeste."

"And how do you think they went about doing that, then?" Officer Miller asked. "Somebody must have patched her through, right?"

"Or they knew her extension number, which is made private for a very good reason. Specifically, this." He motioned to the phone which had been unplugged.

"Do you think somebody from the crew let it leak?" Celeste asked him, turning pale with worry. "I want them vetted."

"Of course," George said. "But I doubt if any of them had anything to do with this. Most likely has something to do with whomever was working the phones today. I'll have Maurice look into it. You just focus on your shoot, okay?" He furrowed his brow as he cupped her cheek. "And see if Carlisle can do something about your hairline. It looks to be receding a little."

Celeste's hand reached automatically for her forehead, her fingers burying themselves into her dark hair, a slight flush spreading on her cheeks. "I'll talk to him," she murmured, then turned back to the officer. "Fine whoever did this, please," she said. "I don't want to deal with them anymore."

Officer Miller nodded. "Of course, Miss Diaz," he said. "But I'm not sure how much I can do. We get thousands of cases like this every day, especially living here in Los Angeles. You're not the only celebrity receiving threatening phone calls."

"But she will be one less," George growled in the officer's direction. "Or we will sue the city. Do you understand?"

Officer Miller's eyes widened and he nodded, swallowing hard. "Yes sir," he said. He looked to Celeste. "We'll get to the bottom of this, Ma'am," he promised.

"Thank you," Celeste replied, then turned and walked back to her vanity, dismissing him with the wave of her hand. Immediately, Amanda and Carlisle, who'd shown up around the same time Officer Miller had, were upon her. They whispered soothing words to her as they got started on her hair and makeup, making her look presentable for her next magazine cover.

And, as duplicitous as she had felt earlier, Celeste felt grateful for the mask of makeup, the disguise of a wig. This was the best way, she decided internally as she took a deep breath, to hide her worry from the world.

To hide her fear.

Chapter Three

After over twelve hours spent in front of the camera, Celeste had all but forgotten about the mysterious phone call from that morning. By the time she was permitted to leave and grab a late dinner (which would be the only substantial thing she'd eaten all day) she had convinced herself that it was just a prank call, done by somebody who was smart enough to charm his way through the switchboards. Nothing more would come of it, obviously.

Still, she found herself searching through Google on her phone for a bodyguard. Somebody who was strong, agile, and easy for her to put her trust in. She stayed in her dressing room an extra hour until she'd found the perfect person and sent their profile off to George to conduct an interview and make the hire. She wanted them on staff as soon as possible and even offered to pay them a generous salary from her own pocket if George was feeling a little frugal.

When she was finally ready to leave, Celeste enlisted two of the security guards to escort her to her car. Their names, she remembered, were Danny and Sugar (whose moniker was, apparently, given to him because of the pure white appearance of his hair despite his dark skin) and they were the two largest men on the security team. And, incidentally, the sweetest.

As they walked through the studio to the parking lot, Danny showed her pictures of his own teenaged daughter and Sugar interjected with stories of his five—three of whom, he told her, had the same white-haired condition as he.

"It looks better on them, though," he laughed. "Especially since they all look like their mother."

By the time they had reached her car, Celeste found herself completely relaxed and the memory of the voice on the phone was distant, almost completely gone. Replaced with Danny's impression of his daughter's stuttering boyfriend and Sugar's thundering laugh. Celeste almost wished that she could steal them away from the studio for her own team, but they were both contracted for at least the next year and she wouldn't take that security away from them for a threat that could possibly just be nothing.

She just let herself relax in their presence, pulling out her keys as they got closer to her parking spot and clicking the button on the tiny remote. The lights of her Mercedes flashed a half dozen spots away and they picked up the pace a little, still laughing. The sound of their voices reverberated around them, but then suddenly stopped when they were close enough to see her back windshield. Celeste's breath froze in her lungs and the keys dropped from her hand, clattering to the ground. In the silence, it sounded like the explosion of a bomb.

Written in deep, red...whatever (Celeste didn't even want to know what it was) were the words, "I'M REALLY GOING TO KILL YOU" in large, block letters, threatening her from her own car. Celeste immediately turned all around, fear gripping her heart at the sight of a dozen darkened corners, any of which could be concealing her harasser. She felt herself get pulled back and screamed, before a hand was thrown over her mouth and a familiar voice whispered in her ear.

"Calm down, Miss Diaz," Danny said. "It's just us. We're calling the cops and taking you back inside. Everything's going to be alright, Miss. We won't let anything happen to you."

Try as she might—and she did try, forcing herself to move with them, back into the safeguarded building—Celeste couldn't allow herself to believe their words. Not with that threat painted on her car, glaring at her back as she was led away.

Chapter Four

They told her that everything was fine. That they had a suspect in mind and they just needed a little more evidence to book him. They told her that, by tomorrow morning, she would be completely safe.

But, just in case, the studio booked her a hotel suite nearby. Not that it was at all necessary, no. Of course not. It was more of a...a gift, they told her; something to apologize for all that she'd gone through that day. George had rolled his eyes, but escorted her to his own town car and held her trembling body all the way to the hotel.

"Everything's gonna be alright, kid," he promised, his voice as gruff as usual.

At the hotel, George was sure to keep Celeste's identity a secret, which wasn't so hard when she wasn't wearing any makeup. He also gave her a hat, sweater, and a pair of sunglasses (none of which were in style, she noted) and checked her in. Her room was on the seventh floor.

When they arrived, there was a woman in a suit waiting for them, her face tan and steely, her body long and lithe, her arms muscular (from what Celeste could tell).

"Good evening, Miss Diaz," she greeted. "My name is Ramona Cruz; I'm your new bodyguard."

Celeste turned to George with wide eyes. "You called her already?" she asked.

"As soon as I got the email from you," he affirmed. "I figured it was a big deal if you actually wanted to hire somebody. You've been against getting a bodyguard since I met you. Then, when you called me about the threat you got tonight, I decided the sooner Ms. Cruz starts, the better. She comes highly recommended."

"I was Special Forces," Ramona informed Celeste. "I've been working security since I finished my second tour. I promise I'll protect you will all that I have, Ma'am."

"Um, you can call me Celeste. I'm not big on the whole 'ma'am' thing."

Ramona nodded. "Then you may call me Cruz."

"Cruz," Celeste said, nodding. "Nice to meet you." She held out her hand and Ramona grasped it, shaking firmly.

"Likewise, Miss—Celeste. I'm a fan."

"You are?" Celeste groaned internally.

"I've seen a few of your more artsy shots; they're very good."

"Well, that's mostly the photographers."

"Without something to shoot, a photographer's work is meaningless."

"Very true."

"Now that you're both acquainted," George interrupted, "let's get you settled. Tomorrow's shoot has been cancelled and you're not to leave the room until I come to get you, alright?"

"Fine with me," Celeste sighed. "It's about time I get a little break."

"You went on a month-long vacation not too long ago!" George argued.

"George, you can *hardly* call that a vacation. I did at least two beach shoots a week."

"But you got yourself a nice tan," he retorted. "And you made us both a pretty penny, didn't ya? So quit your complaining and enjoy the time off while you got it, okay?" Celeste rolled her eyes, but couldn't fight the grin that sprung up on her face. "Now give me a hug and go to bed. I'll be back tomorrow to check up on you and give you a couple of updates."

Celeste did as she was told, wrapping her arms around George's bulky body. He really was like a father to her; always protective. "I'll see you tomorrow," she murmured into his collar.

He patted her gently on the back and pulled away, giving her a long look, before he nodded and made his way to the door. Before he left, he turned to Ramona, who stood, still as a statue, next to the entrance.

"You keep her safe," he said. At Ramona's curt nod, he walked out.

"Are you going to stand there all night?" Celeste asked her bodyguard.

"Not all night," Ramona replied. "Just until I get the alright from the hotel security. They have the entire building under surveillance, checking each floor for any signs of suspicious activity. When I get the call, I'll go to sleep."

"Okay," Celeste said. "Well...good night, Cruz."

"Sweet dreams, Celeste."

Chapter Five

Celeste didn't sleep that night. Every single sound—the creak of a floorboard, the whistle of the wind, the drip of a faucet—kept her awake, kept her alert. She stayed huddled beneath her blankets, feeling the seconds tick by with the rhythm of her heart until the sun began to rise above the horizon.

Then there was a knock at the door.

"Celeste?" Ramona's voice came through, loud and far too awake for being so early in the morning.

"Yes?" Celeste groaned, burrowing into her pillow.

"I ordered breakfast if you're hungry. And coffee." That was the magic word that had Celeste shoving the sheets down her body and slipping out of bed, throwing on the sinfully soft robe that the hotel had provided. Ramona was waiting for her at the door and handed her a warm mug. "Skinny vanilla latte," she said, smiling.

"How did you know?" Celeste asked, inhaling the rich scent of Colombian Dark Roast deeply.

"George gave a whole list of your likes and dislikes, in case we ended up working together for an extended period of time."

"Hopefully not," Celeste said. "Not that you're not great, but...I'm not really all that okay with having somebody following me everywhere I go. Especially stalkers and bodyguards. No offense."

"I get it," Ramona agreed. "Privacy can be a wonderful thing. It's something that I've grown quite fond of since I got back to the States."

"You didn't have much overseas?" Celeste asked her as she sat down at the dining room table, in front of a verifiable buffet of all her favorite foods.

"None at all," Ramona sighed. "We were all packed into one tent like sardines. Barely enough room to stretch out your legs unless you wanted to go outside, where the heat was unbearable. Except at night, when you practically froze to death. Yeah, it was a lot of fun, the desert."

Celeste chuckled. "Well, thank you for your service, anyway, Cruz," she said. "I do appreciate it."

"So do I," Ramona laughed. "I was never this fit before I signed up."

They laughed together this time and soon both were enjoying their continental breakfasts. Until Celeste finished hers and started feeling even more tired than before, her eyes beginning to droop despite the three cups of coffee she'd drank.

"Celeste, are you okay?" Ramona asked, looking worried.

"I'm find," Celeste yawned. "I just didn't get any sleep last night."

"Do you want to rest for a while?" Ramona asked. "I can take watch again. I'll make sure nothing hurts you."

"Honestly," Celeste said. "That would be so great." She yawned again and stood, making her way over to the couch in the living room and flopping down, her face landing on an incredibly soft pillow. She let out a deep sigh as she felt herself finally succumb to the pull of sleep.

When she woke, nearly three hours later, she felt much better and was able to stretch her limbs out, feeling her muscles loosen and her joints release whatever built up tension they held. Ramona was propped up against the sofa near her feet, absorbed in a rather heavy duty book.

"Hey," Celeste croaked, her voice thick with sleep. "What time is it?"

"Nearly eleven," Ramona replied, checking her watch. "You were out all morning."

"Oh," Celeste sighed. "Wow. I haven't slept this late since...ever, I think. It felt kind of nice."

"That's good," Ramona said. "Oh, and George called while you were sleeping. He said to call him back as soon as you can."

"Maybe he has some updates," Celeste murmured as she stood and made her way back into her bedroom. Her phone was lying on the bedside table, right where she left it the night before. She plucked it off and dialed the familiar number (George's and her mother's were the only numbers Celeste knew by heart).

The phone rang twice before he answered. "Celeste?"

"Hey, George," she greeted. "What's up?"

"I'm so glad you called back," George said. "We have a lead on the maniac. Security cameras caught a glimpse of him in the parking structure yesterday. They don't have a face yet, but he was driving an old beat up Jeep with the plates covered."

"Then how are you going to find it?" Celeste asked, sighing.

"There's a ding just above the right brake light," George informed her. "The cops are going to use that to track him down. I just wanted to let you know."

"Thanks, George," Celeste sighed. "And thanks for giving Cruz that list of things for me. It's making staying here a lot more bearable."

There was a long silence, then:

"List? What list?"

Before Celeste could say anything more, everything went black.

Chapter Six

When Celeste came to, everything was still black, but she could feel herself moving. She was in the back of a car and there was music in her ears. Her eyes, she could feel, were covered by a blindfold. Her hair was being ruffled by wind and she could feel her body still encased in the fluffy bathrobe from before.

"Where am I?" she growled out, her voice hoarse, as if her throat was filled with gravel.

"Oh great," she heard a familiar voice say. "You're awake." She heard the soft whir of a motor and then there was no more wind.

"Cruz?" Celeste gasped. "What the...what are you doing?"

"What does it look like?" Ramona snapped. "I'm rescuing you."

"*Rescuing me*? From *what*?"

"From George!" Ramona groaned. "He's been planning some pretty horrible things. I've been hired to keep an eye on you; that's why I planted those threats."

"You're the one who's been threatening me?"

"Yes," Ramona said. "But not without reason."

"I'm waiting..." Celeste said, after a moment of silence.

"Your manager's been planning to get rid of you," Ramona informed her and Celeste was, understandably dubious. "He's done the same with his last three clients, once they've gotten 'too old'. Typically, they end up committing suicide or go off to some mysterious rehab facility and are never seen again. But you...you were going to turn up dead."

"How the hell do you know that?"

"I've been assigned to watch him since his last client went missing a decade ago. We found her body last month, in a landfill."

"I never heard anything about this," Celeste said.

"Yeah, we planned it that way," Ramona sighed. "Lest he decide to move on win his plans a little more quickly than anticipated. It became clear, over the last week, that preparations were in order to make sure you were…for lack of a better term, I'll just say whacked. He already had deals with a local mobster. That's where I come in."

"But, wait," Celeste said. "I found you online. I chose you from thousands of applicants."

"Because I planted my profile there," Ramona informed her. "I actually planted several personas there, just in case, but you chose that one. Ramona Cruz."

"So that's not your real name then?"

"No. And you're not going to get my real name, either," she said. "Not until we're far away and I can make sure you're safe. So long as George thinks you've been kidnapped by a crazed fan, you are. Even better if he thinks you're dead; less work for him."

"But where am I going to go?" Celeste asked. "And what about my mom? And my career?"

"All gone now. We were able to siphon half of your wealth into an account in your new name, but, for the most part, you're no longer Celeste Diaz or even Celestina, anymore."

"Who am I, then?"

"We'll talk more about that when we get where we're going," Not-Ramona promised. "For now, just sit back and relax as your entire world changes around you. Everything will be different, sure, but you'll have a better life. I promise."

PREMONITION

RICHARD POCHE

CHAPTER ONE

Jaimi dreamed about her son.

Dominic. A rambunctious five year old that can't stop running around the house. He had a head full of brown curls and a smile that made even the grumpiest of old ladies melt.

She dreamed about him racing up and down the driveway in his little mini-car. They had bought the toy for him on his fourth birthday. He inherited the love of cars from his father. They watched NASCAR together and collected Hot Wheels.

Like father, like son.

But the dream shifted as Dominic pretended to shift gears on his little mini-Mustang.

He looked older now. In his early twenties, driving like a maniac down the street.

A young woman sat on the passenger side. The two appeared to be arguing but their words came out garbled in Jaimi's nightmare.

The young woman gesticulated with a violent fervor, pointing her finger in Dominic's face as he tried to keep his eyes on the road.

Jaimi's son yelled at her, pushing her away.

Their voices muffled, they yelled at each other like trapped animals.

The young woman then reached over and turned the steering wheel into oncoming traffic. Jaimi heard horns blaring, tires squealing and the smashing of metal at high speeds.

She watched as her son's car rolled over several times.

Dominic coughed and writhed in pain, blood streaming down the side of his face like a dying soldier. A cross necklace dangled from the rear window. A gold chain topped by a handcrafted painting of Jesus on a cross.

The sound of the horn echoing through the night.

"Mommy!"

Jaimi bolted awake to see Dominic jumping on her bed.

"Are we still going?"

"Going where?"

"You said you'd take me to the park," Dominic leaped off the mattress and began doing a shimmy dance of his own creation.

"Right, right," Jaimi slipped out of the bed, covered with the thin blanket.

"What's wrong?"

"Nothing," Jaimi said, tousling her child's hair. "Mommy just had a bad dream, that's all."

Jaimi showered, letting the water scratch fingernails down her body as she tried to forget the nightmare. She laughed to herself as Dominic had already cleaned his room, fed the cat and dressed.

"Are you ready yet?" he called out from behind the bathroom door.

"You're going to have to wait," she said. "Patience is a virtue. Remember that when Mommy is getting ready. Or doing anything else."

They walked to the park. Or she walked and he drove in his mini-Mustang. The toy car didn't travel more than two miles an hour as Dominic flipped a lever and watched as the windshield wipers battled pretend rain.

Jaimi looked up at the cloudless sky and already felt the sun beating down. She began to sweat, feeling the moisture gathering under her arms and back.

Dominic pressed down on the horn every five seconds. Then he turned on the radio of the car and it pumped out Kenny G music. Jaimi wondered which one sounded worse.

"Hi," an old man wearing a paint-stained baseball cap said, waving hello at her and the boy. "Young man, that's a nice ride you got there."

"Thank you, sir," Dominic said, honking the horn.

The old man looked over at Jaimi and laughed at the cuteness of the boy. She watched her son scoot along in his mini-car, listening to the birds chirp in the trees above as if they were performing an opera celebrating a perfect day.

She cherished moments like this, working two twelve-hour shifts on weekends in order to spend the rest of her time with Dominic. If she had her druthers, she would spend all of her time with her son, leaving the zoo of stupidity at work to her co-workers who deserved it.

Her son honked his horn again but the noise spurred a memory of her dream last night.

Jaimi closed her eyes, remembering the twenty-something Dominic spinning over and over in the car.

Car horns echoing through her head.

Then she remembered entering a graveyard.

"Our Mother of Sorrows" read the sign at the entrance.

Venturing inside, she saw a group of people milling around a headstone.

A marker that bore the name of her son, Dominic.

Two women in matching blue dresses looked up at Jaimi, eyes hot and puffy, then back down at the headstones. The younger of the two had two bouquets of flowers, placing one on Dominic's grave and the other on the headstone next to his.

"Mommy!" Dominic called out, tugging at Jaimi's pant legs. "Can we go to McDonald's?"

"Sure," she said, snapping out of her daydream. "Sure, why not."

Jaimi threw out the remains of Dominic's half-eaten *Happy Meal,* then looked out the window to see him playing in the garage driveway.

"Vroom! Vroom!" the boy called out even though the mini-Mustang replicated the sounds of a real car. "Out of the way, out of the way!"

Feeling sleepy, Jaimi trudged over to the sofa and laid down. Rolling over, her eyes caught the picture on the coffee table. Dominic, her ex-husband Ian and herself all posing for the camera in happier times.

What happened?

She met Ian in church but didn't really get to know him until they attended a beach wedding of a mutual friend. They talked, joked and flirted with each other all to the beat of a beach surf supplying a metronome.

Everything seemed perfect and meant to be.

Predestined.

Closing her eyes, Jaimi felt her head go deeper into the pillow as she drifted into sleep.

Then her nightmare started again.

She saw Dominic, writhing in pain inside the vehicle. He struggled to catch his breath, coughing up blood.

The car horn continued to blare as he began reaching out, up toward the cross necklace dangling in front of him.

"Mommy!"

Jaimi woke up, feeling Dominic's hands pushing against her body.

"Why aren't you out playing?" she groaned.

"Did you have another bad dream?"

"Yeah," Jaimi said, sitting up. "How did you know?"

"You were talking in your sleep."

"What did I say?"

"You called out my name," he said. "Did you have a bad dream about me?"

"No. No, of course not."

Jaimi noticed that Dominic had a necklace around his neck. The cross pendant identical to the one she saw dangling from the rear-view mirror in her dream.

"Where did you get this?" Jaimi asked, fingering the jewelry.

"Dad gave it to me," Dominic said.

"When?"

"Last week," he said. "He told me it would bring me good luck."

CHAPTER TWO

"I don't like the weekend deal," Ian said, feeling like a stranger in his former home.

"Neither do I," Jaimi stuffed a pair of little boy pants into a backpack.

"So why are we doing this?" Ian held up his arms. He looked at Jaimi with a patented look of wide-incredulity that she hated so much during their marriage.

Ian stood tall and had a stentorian voice to match. He always made sure that the volume of his words rose higher than those of the person he argued with. Something he picked up from his father.

They were both preacher men.

Ian inherited the pastoral duties at United Methodist Church in Oakland after the retirement of his father seven years ago.

He married Jaimi and they had put up a false front for the family and the church for a few years. But they kept fighting. And fighting. Until-

"Because we're divorced. Remember?"

Ian sighed hard, looking around the house. "I didn't know it was going to be like this."

"Be like what?" Jaimi asked. "We talked and talked. We went to counseling. We tried-"

"Maybe you didn't try hard enough."

She turned around and stared. Her eyes like knives.

"Okay, fine," Ian said. "Maybe we didn't try hard enough."

Jaimi clenched her fists. "You know, I'm not going to go through this every time-"

"Fine. I'll stop," Ian said, holding up his palms in a placating gesture. "You ready to go, Champ?"

"Almost," Dominic called out from his bedroom. "Patience is a virtue."

"What?" Ian laughed.

"Be sure and brush your teeth," Jaimi said.

Ian took out his cell phone and began thumbing through the screens, trying to do anything to distract himself.

Jaimi watched. She knew that Ian did that when he wanted to tune the world out. She sighed and wondered if she should tell him at all.

"Ian?"

"Yeah," he said, looking up from his cell phone.

"There's something I've been wanting to tell you."

"Okay."

"I've been having these dreams," she said. "Premonitions."

"Premonitions?"

"Figured that you might be the one man that wouldn't think I'm crazy. You know, your Dad used to always preach about those things."

"You mean his visions?" Ian suppressed a laugh. "He had to use those in his sermons to, you know, buttress a point sometimes."

"Mine are real."

"Okay-"

"Just like when my Dad died," Jaimi sat down on the couch. "You know, I had that dream of him dying in a car crash. Then it came true."

"It wasn't a vision," Ian said, sitting down next to her. "It was a coincidence."

Jaimi shook her head, gathering her thoughts. "I didn't see it that way."

"I think it's your imagination."

"So all of those stories in the Bible. All of those stories that people have of hearing God directing them-"

"Imagination," Ian said. "They believe they hear something that they really don't. Imagination is a powerful thing. People hear something in a sermon, they read the stories and they can create voices and scenarios in their head. Your brain is a ventriloquist. Your dreams are your fears talking. Not God."

"You don't know that."

"I've spent my whole life around that sort of thing. I know."

"I'm going to take a drive today," Jaimi said. "Go to the graveyard called Our Mother of Sorrows. Think it is off Piedmont Avenue. It is where they will bury Dominic. That much I know."

"What?" Ian stood up.

"I know you think I'm crazy," Jaimi said. "But I saw it in my dream. He is much older. Maybe in his early twenties. Then there was this girl. Woman. They go off the side of the road and hit a car head-on."

Ian remained silent for what felt like several minutes.

"You saw Dominic die?" he finally asked.

Jaimi nodded. "Only he was older."

"I don't want to hear about this stuff," Ian said. "My mom was the same way. Said she had all of these prophetic dreams and talked about them as if they were real. They weren't. Drove my Dad crazy."

"So you think I'm crazy?"

"I think you're obsessing about something that you shouldn't obsess about. You fear losing Dominic. I do too. So it manifests itself in a dream."

The boy stepped out of the hallway and looked up at his father.

"Ready?" Ian asked. "It is off to the zoo we go."

"Can mommy come?"

"Maybe next time," Ian said, ushering the boy to the front door.

Jaimi looked out the window Dominic hopped into the driver side of Ian's car. She wanted Dominic to turn around and see her watching through the window.

To wave goodbye.

But they just drove away.

Jaimi spent half the day meandering through the gravestones. She began to feel silly after a few hours, looking for a "sign" like some religious lunatic.

Hungry, she left the graveyard and began looking for a place to eat. She liked the town of Piedmont with their main street showcase of local artisans, antique shops, and ethnic restaurants.

Jaimi opted for the mom and pop diner, deciding to reward herself with a cheeseburger and fries. The hostess introduced herself as Iris and escorted Jaimi to a table by the window.

Her waiter, a man whose name tag read Timothy, had been attentive throughout. He had slate blue eyes and a bit of a stubble which she didn't like but she found him handsome nonetheless.

"Anything else, I can get you?" he took her empty glass off the table and traced the edge as if touching a woman's body.

"No," Jaimi said. "It was delicious. Thank you."

"No problem," Timothy looked at her funny again. "Sorry, but I know you. You are the wife of Pastor-"

"Ian McDonnell," she said.

"That's right. The Methodist church, right?"

"That's right."

"My mom used to go to that church," Timothy said. "I went there a few times with her."

"Really?" Jaimi squinted her eyes, trying to place Timothy. "I don't remember you. It's a big church, though. So we really don't have an opportunity to meet everyone."

"No worries," Timothy said. "Mom went there almost every week."

"What does she look like?"

The young man took out his cell phone. He flipped through a few screens and then turned the device around to show Jaimi. "Nancy."

Jaimi gasped.

The woman resembled one of the women in her dreams. The older of the two who were wearing blue dresses at the grave-site.

"I remember her," Jaimi said, telling a half-truth. She scrutinized the picture of his mother, a pockmarked face woman with graying hair pulled back like the Bride of Frankenstein. "How is she?"

"Doing good," Timothy said. "Still working at the clinic"

"The clinic?"

"Breast center," Timothy said. "Does mammograms. Big brown house by the lake. Converted it into a clinic."

"Know it," Jaimi said, realizing she found the sign she had been looking for.

CHAPTER THREE

Ian blamed himself for the dissolution of his marriage.

He did not date much before he met Jaimi. He felt cursed, feeling as if he had been born guilty, that he had done something unforgivable that he didn't know about.

He believed that he had inherited this mental ailment from his father but couldn't pinpoint the reasons why.

"Sinners look different," his father used to say to him. "Just look closely and you'll see it. You'll know it. Especially when you look in the mirror."

Ian wanted to be different from his dad, to not live a life running from imaginary curses.

His conversation with Jaimi made him remember how his own father used to talk about experiencing apocalyptic visions and personalized messages from God. He incorporated them into his sermons, manipulating his flock into believing he had a direct line to the Almighty.

His father would start his sermons off in a quiet and pleasant voice but after thirty minutes he would be soaked in sweat. Ian remembered his father pointing at his congregation with a long finger which shook from early Alzheimer's, eyeballing every member like a dinosaur stalking little men with spears.

But Ian had a completely different preaching style. He knew the younger audience wouldn't be into the verbal tongue lashings of his father's time. He did use some of the same warnings against moral decay in his sermons like his dad did but without the supernatural fire and brimstone. Ian prepared his messages so that they focused more on being a good person while avoiding a lot of the paranormal elements of the Bible.

He didn't believe in visions or premonitions.

Until he had the nightmare himself.

About his son Dominic.

Ian tossed and turned in bed, seeing Dominic as a young man, just as Jaimi had described. He watched as now college-aged son got into his car with a young woman, holding the door open for her.

They drove through the city, increasing their speed. They argued. He couldn't hear what they were saying.

Suddenly, the young woman reached over and they slammed into another car headed in the opposite direction.

Ian shuddered awake.

And saw Dominic standing by his bedside.

"Do you have bad dreams too, Daddy?"

"Sometimes."

"I heard you talking in your sleep. Calling my name."

"Everyone has bad dreams," Ian said. "But they're just dreams. They're not real. You wake up and realize that they not real and then it comes as a relief, right?"

"It's scary sometimes," the boy said.

"How about some hot chocolate?" Ian asked. "Do you think that will make the bad dreams go away?"

Dominic's face lit up, nodding in agreement. He turned around and raced toward the kitchen.

Ian got up to follow but not before he picked up his cell phone off the bedside table.

He texted Jaimi.

"I need to see you."

Jaimi had her doctor refer her to Nancy's clinic for a mammogram. She felt like a blessed detective, getting lucky enough to have Timothy's mother perform her mammogram.

Everything looked in order and Jaimi found Nancy to be an all too enthusiastic informant.

"Yeah, I stopped going to the church a little after your husband's dad retired," Nancy said as she escorted Jaimi back to waiting room. "I like the fire and brimstone stuff. Your husband was a little too milquetoast for me. No offense."

"We're divorced now," Jaimi said.

"Sorry," Nancy said. "But they all end in divorce. Like me and my husband. Should have never married his ass but I did anyway. Now my boy is making the same mistake. I wish he had met someone like you. A nice, Christian woman."

"Thanks," Jaimi said. "Yes, you've raised a nice, young man. I met him at the diner."

"He's getting married next week," Nancy said. "Idiot. Getting married in this day and age. Been shacked up for two years with that hussy."

"Oh," Jaimi said, not knowing what else to offer.

"You are in shape," Nancy said. "He'd be better off with you. That slut of his is gonna end up just like me. I gotta lose weight."

Nancy grabbed at her fat stomach then sucked in her gut. "What kind of diet are you on? Paleo? Weight Watchers? I've tried everything. None of those fad diets work for me."

"I just run a lot," Jaimi said. "Chase after my little boy."

"My son needs to marry someone like you."

"That's very nice. Thank you."

Nancy looked behind herself and lowered her voice to a conspiratorial tone. "His girlfriend is a slut. A whore! Her morality done left the building and took a permanent vacation. I have dreams about her. I dream of taking this giant sponge and wiping her off the face of the earth like the stain that she is."

"Sorry to hear that," Jaimi said.

"Look at this shit," Nancy took out her cell phone and showed Jaimi a picture. "You can see it in her face. Evil thoughts can't stay hidden. They just can't. Her mother is the same way. Used to go to school with her. She's a slut too."

Jaimi scrutinized the picture. She immediately recognized Timothy's fiancee as the younger woman in her dream. The one that placed the bouquet of flowers on her son's gravestone.

"What's her name?"

"I call her Hellcat," Nancy laughed. "But her real name is Micaela. What the hell kind of name is that?"

"What does she do?"

"She doesn't do shit," Nancy said. "Sits on her ass at the gun shop at the end of the block. Her parents own the place. She just sits there at the cash register, spends all day farting and flirting."

CHAPTER FOUR

The bell rang as Jaimi stepped through the door of the dimly lit gun shop. A lake of sawdust and broken glass greeted her at the entrance but she tip-toed through the mess.

Jaimi meandered through the store, feigning interest at the guns behind the glass casing.

At the side wall, she saw a picture of Micaela holding up a gun.

Closing her eyes, a vision came to her mind as if from divine origin.

Jaimi saw Micaela grieving at the graveyard again. She saw a headstone with her son Dominic's name written across. Then she watched as Micaela placed a wreath on the grave next to his.

The inscription read "Fiona Parker. Forever our little girl."

"Sorry about the mess," the voice behind her said. "We had a break in and changing some things around. Can I help you with something?"

Jaimi turned around startled.

"Micaela?"

"Yes," the woman said, swatting at some bugs that flew around a lantern on the counter.

"I'm Jaimi."

"I'm sorry," Micaela's eyes bulged out in curiosity. Fair skinned, she wore a spaghetti-strapped blouse which showed off sunburned shoulders. "Do I know you?"

"No," Jaimi said. "But. Do you have a daughter? A daughter named Fiona?"

"No," the woman laughed, rubbing her stomach. "No kids, yet. But we're working on it. I'm getting married next week."

"Congratulations."

"Is that what you came in here to ask me?" Micaela pointed to the guns on the rack.

"No," Jaimi stammered. "No."

"Well, can I interest you in something for home defense?" Micaela asked. "Or hunting? Or both, shit, some guns can work both ways if you catch my drift."

"No," Jaimi said. "No, I was just looking around. Thanks very much."

Jaimi walked out of the gun shop, tipping over a container of bullets but catching them before they fell.

"Are you alright?" Micaela asked.

"I'm fine," Jaimi said, rushing through the door. "Fine."

CHAPTER FIVE

Ian arrived at Jaimi's residence and knocked on the door. He didn't care that he came over unannounced. She didn't answer his texts. Maybe something was wrong? Maybe she was ignoring him like she did when she was mad.

He realized how one of the primary problems in his marriage was that he never truly understood his wife. He remembered how he never got used to her moods and how after their fights he would often dream like he was a kite.

A kite floating in the air with no one holding the string.

Vulnerable to the wind just as he became vulnerable to her moods.

He never knew what she would do next.

"Hi," Jaimi opened the door, looking surprised.

"Hi."

"What are you doing here?"

"You won't answer my texts," Ian said, letting himself in.

"Where's Dominic?"

"I dropped him off at my folks," Ian took a deep breath as he looked around the place he once called home. Artwork of their son dotted the walls. Yogurt colored paintings, intense with a child's passion. A window to innocent places. "You didn't get my text?"

"Been busy," Jaimi shrugged her shoulders.

"Look, about what you said earlier. About the dreams."

"Yeah."

"I believe you."

Jaimi cocked her head at Ian, trying to read his face. "If you're just saying that-"

"No," Ian said. "Believe me. I had the same dream. I dreamed of Dominic in a car. And this girl takes control of the wheel."

"That's what I told you."

"She had blonde hair. Green eyes. Pretty."

"Okay."

"And he had a cross necklace hanging from the dash. The one I gave him."

Jaimi's eyes almost bugged out of her head. "And what else?"

"They drove a red Mustang."

"Impossible," Jaimi said, running her fingers through her hair. "Can't be."

"Am I right?"

Jaimi nodded.

"What do you think we should do?" Ian asked.

"I have to prevent the girl from being born. Prevent the killer of our son to ever set foot on his earth. I have to prevent that."

"You mean we," Ian corrected. "We have to prevent the girl from being born."

Jaimi waited outside the gun store in her car, blasting the radio so she could drown out the fears that danced in her head.

Waiting for Micaela to leave the store, she exited out of her vehicle when she saw the lights being shut off inside. Within moments, Micaela stepped out the door.

"Micaela?"

"Yeah," the woman looked up with a wariness in her eye.

"I just want to apologize for the way I came across earlier," Jaimi said. "I know I must have sounded crazy."

"No worries," Micaela said, reaching into her purse and taking out a pack of cigarettes. She offered one to Jaimi who shook her head.

"I know it sounded crazy," Jaimi said. "But I had a dream about my father. A few years back. I dreamed about him dying in a car crash. The next morning, he did."

"Sorry to hear that," Micaela said, walking to her car. A beat-up Nissan Sentra with stickers of Heavy Metal bands all across the back bumper.

"Now I'm dreaming that you are going to have a daughter that will be named Fiona," Jaimi said with dramatic certainty. "And she will kill my son."

"What?"

"It was a premonition," Jaimi said. "I had a dream. I saw you at the grave site of my son and your daughter."

"Holy shit," Micaela laughed, revealing yellow teeth and a diseased gum line. "You are fucking nuts."

Micaela opened her driver side door but Jaimi pushed it closed.

"Where's Timothy?"

"What?"

"He must know," Jaimi said. "Maybe you and he could talk things out. You know, just wait a little longer before you-"

"Fuck off," Micaela said, shoving Jaimi back with her right hand. "That isn't any of your business."

"He deserves better than you," Jaimi said. "And you know it."

"Excuse me?"

"He belongs with me," Jaimi sneered.

"Look, you are about the craziest bitch that I've ever seen," Micaela pushed Jaimi down, her accuser hitting the asphalt hard. "Come at me again and I'll finish your ass."

"Wait," Jaimi muttered.

"Wait, nothing."

Micaela dropped her cigarette down on Jaimi's blouse and she felt the ashes burn into her skin.

CHAPTER SIX

Jaimi lurked around the burger diner, seeing if Timothy was on duty but she saw only Iris.

She googled Timothy's full name, toggling through the "White Pages" listings on the Internet before she stumbled on his address.

Jaimi found his apartment within twenty minutes. He had a first-floor unit, his door hidden from the street by a tree. He rolled up in a dented white Jeep Cherokee. Stepping out of his car, he looked surprised to see her.

"Jaimi?"

"Timothy," she said in her most comforting voice. "I have to talk to you."

"Okay."

"You can't go through with it."

"Go through with what?"

"The wedding."

"We have rehearsals tomorrow."

"You can't marry Micaela."

"Why?" he tilted his head, beady eyes shimmering with curiosity.

"She's no good for you, Timothy," Jaimi said. "Look, I know that it is none of my business but I can see it in your eyes. You're not a man in love. You're a man settling. Trust me I've seen that look before."

"But you don't even know me."

"I know men," Jaimi said. "I can tell you are faking it. If you listen to me I can spare you a lifetime of hurt."

Timothy turned his back to Jaimi. He placed his hands on his hips and began pacing back and forth. "You need to go away."

Jaimi spun him back around. "Look at me," she said. "I need you to think about something."

Blinking her eyes and gulping hard, she took Timothy's right hand and placed it on her breast.

"There is so much more out there for you," she said, her voice now soft and sexy. "So much more. You haven't been with enough women to know. You haven't lived yet. You're going to throw it all away on someone who isn't worth it."

Timothy pulled his hand away.

"What are you-"

"Just think about it," Jaimi said, heading back to her vehicle.

Jaimi tried meditating before she went to sleep that night. She logged onto Youtube and listened to some ASMR videos to calm her mind.

She couldn't stand dreaming about her son dying again.

Drifting into sleep, the young woman popped up in the dream first. Fiona.

She screamed at Dominic.

"You can't do this to me!"

"All we do is fight," Dominic said. "We're not right for each other."

"I'm not going to let you do this to me!" the young woman screamed, reaching over and taking the wheel.

A church bell rang.

Jaimi jolted up.

The church bells ringing in her head.

Squinting in the morning light, Jaimi put on a baseball cap, t-shirt, and blue jeans before heading out of the door.

She got into her car and ran several red lights before skidding to a halt in front of the Catholic church.

Running inside, she saw Timothy and Micaela walking down the aisle. Timothy's best man, Simon, stood behind him as a priest directed them to come forward. Iris from the restaurant stood to the side of Micaela.

"No!" Jaimi said. "It can't happen!"

She sprinted toward the couple before the priest caught her by the arm.

"Get the hell off me!" Jaimi pushed the elderly clergyman and he staggered backward, falling into the pews. "You don't get it. This marriage cannot happen!"

"Goddamnit!" Micaela tossed down her bouquet and headed straight for Jaimi. The two women locked arms, grabbing at each other like octopuses before Timothy and his best man separated them.

"You can't do it, Timothy!" Jaimi said. "Stay away from her!"

"I'll call the police!" the priest said.

"No," Timothy said, pushing Jaimi backward. "No."

"We need to call the cops," the priest said again, wide-eyed in fear.

"It's okay," Timothy said, leading Jaimi out of the church. "I got this."

Once outside the building, Timothy placed his hands on both of Jaimi's shoulders. "You can't do this, okay?"

"You can't marry her," Jaimi said, nearly in tears.

"I don't even know you," Timothy said. "You're acting crazy."

"You will have a daughter," Jaimi said. "And she will kill my son."

"Go home, Jaimi," Timothy said. "If you don't leave, I will call the cops."

CHAPTER SEVEN

Jaimi laid on her back on the sofa. Leaning over, she stared out her front window as if waiting for a sign from God.

"You can't be serious," Ian said looking down at his ex-wife as she held a pistol in her lap.

Jaimi sat up and put a clip in the gun. "They don't believe me. Nobody believes me. It's a crazy story. What other choice is there?"

"You do that, you go to jail," Ian said. "Duh. Then Dominic doesn't have a mother."

"If I don't do it then he doesn't have a life."

"Look," Ian stood in front of Jaimi and placed his hand on the gun, pushing the weapon down. "I'm with you. Okay? I'm with you. But there has to be some other way."

"I can't keep them apart," Jaimi said. "So one of them has to die."

Ian removed the gun from her hand and took the clip out. He then placed the gun in the bottom drawer, under a cluster of his old shirts. "Didn't even know you had bought a gun."

"There's a lot of things you don't know about me."

Ian looked at Jaimi with thoughtfulness in his eyes. He turned to the window and looked out. He saw a man and women walking with a baby carriage in tow.

"I should have tried harder," Ian said. "You know, when you're young you do and say things that you really don't mean. That's the problem with being young. You don't see the big picture yet. I should have been nicer to you. Did things that make you feel like you were less alone."

Ian had his back turned as Jaimi took the gun out of the drawer.

Without warning, she hit her ex-husband over the back of the head with the butt of the gun. He wobbled and she struck him again, knocking him out.

"Sorry, honey," Jaimi said. "But some things I have to do on my own."

Jaimi slammed her front door shut. Jogging over to her car, she started it up.

She had to kill Timothy.

Driving down the road, she saw a red Mustang came up into her rear-view mirror and zip in front of her.

Looking inside the vehicle, she saw a glimpse of young Dominic with his girlfriend.

Jaimi slammed on the gas and followed them down the road. Every time she accelerated the Mustang matched her speed, not allowing her to get closer.

She went through one red light after another until the car parked in front of Timothy's apartment.

Jaimi pulled up behind the vehicle. Gulping hard, she stepped out of her car and walked to the Mustang with halting steps.

Looking inside, she saw nobody. No trace of Dominic or his girlfriend.

Then she heard a car squeal behind her.

Ian.

He stopped his vehicle in the middle of the road and sprang out of the driver seat.

"I know why you're here," he said, dried blood on the side of his face. "You can't."

Jaimi pointed at the red Mustang. "He led me here."

"Who?"

"Dominic," Jaimi began to cry.

Ian stood in shock as he looked at the parked red Mustang.

The same one from his own dream.

CHAPTER EIGHT

Ian watched as Jaimi tossed and turned in her sleep on the couch. He remembered falling in love with her when she joined the church choir. She would sing solos sometimes, her sweet and painful arias echoing throughout the church with a perfect pitch. She would look for him when she would finish her song, her smile taking him at gunpoint.

They dated and married within a year. She colorized his monotone world. She told him he had the sexiest voice she had ever heard or since.

Then he remembered the long days and nights of holding her in his arms as she cried herself to sleep when her father died.

"We just keep losing people," Jaimi would sob as she pressed her head to his chest. She had lost her mother when she was in her teens and the loss of her father left her feeling empty. "We just keep losing and losing and losing. I know more people up in heaven than I do down here."

Their marriage started to disintegrate after her father's death. Jaimi became more distant and irritable.

Ian tried to recapture their spark but failed. He felt like an actor in a movie who was terribly miscast.

After about an hour nap, she rolled over, her eyes adjusting to the low light.

"Bad dreams?" he asked.

"No," she said. "But I feel like I can sleep for another twelve hours."

"I have an idea."

"About?"

"We can alter destiny," Ian said. "When I was in seminary school we studied how the Calvinists believed in predestination. Maybe these visions are a gift. A gift from God to enable us to change our destiny."

"I don't know," Jaimi said. "All I want is for our son to be happy. And alive."

"We move. Simply as that."

"We?"

"We can be a family again," Ian said. "I had a dream. A dream where we watched our son tip-toe down the steps and open his Christmas presents before he was supposed to. I dreamed of us, huddled together in a closet, laughing as we gave him everything he wanted. It is a symbolic dream. It was-"

"Stop," Jaimi took a deep breath and tried not to cry.

Ian stroked his fingers across her cheek. "I love you so much."

"I don't know," Jaimi said, rubbing sad eyes. "All I know is that I have to do whatever it takes to keep my son alive."

"Just think about what I said," Ian said, getting up to leave. "I'll let you rest."

Timothy skipped up the porch steps of Jaimi's home. He looked up at the large house and wondered if he could ever afford a place like this.

Knocking on the door, he waited for a minute before ringing the doorbell repeatedly.

Jaimi answered with a surprised look on her face.

"Timothy?"

"Can we talk?" he asked.

"Sure," she said. "Of course, come on in."

Timothy walked in, hands in his pockets as if he were afraid to touch anything. Then he took them out and fingered a piece of dried food on his shirt, tearing it away like a scab.

"I was thinking," his voice sounding uncertain. "That you are right. I really don't love Micaela."

Jaimi nodded her head as if she knew that fact all along.

"She was a convenience," Timothy said with a melancholic smile. "I never dated much. I was always an outsider. Some people hook up right away. Dive right in. Me, I was a mask and snorkel kind of guy. But with Micaela she just forced me to dive right in. It hurts me now especially because we've been together so long and she's the only serious girlfriend I've ever had. I want to be with other people. To know what that's like. I want to be with you."

"Are you sure?"

Timothy nodded. "I've thought about you. Thought about you for a long time. Do you think about me?"

"Yes," Jaimi said. "Of course."

CHAPTER NINE

Jaimi had lunch with Timothy at a cafe on the outskirts of the city. She sold

him on the romantic notion of ditching their lives altogether. They could start over in Tahoe, Phoenix or Albuquerque. She would liquidate her retirement and they could live off that while they figured out how to reset their lives.

"Pack all your bags," she told him. "I'll pick you up in the morning."

When she arrived at his apartment at dawn, she had butterflies in her chest. Jaimi didn't think the plan all the way through, long-term. She just needed a short term solution of getting him away from Micaela long enough for the whore to get knocked up by someone else.

"I'm ready," Timothy said as he skipped down the steps of his apartment building.

Jaimi smiled until she saw the look on his face. Following his eye-line, she turned around to see Micaela coming at her from behind.

Looking into her bloodshot eyes, Jaimi could not duck in time as the woman took a big swing at her.

Thhhwwaaaap!

The woman smacked her across the face, the force of the blow causing Jaimi's knees to buckle.

"Bitch!"

Jaimi felt Micaela's hand go across her face again, tasting blood.

"Stop!" Timothy yelled.

"Shut the fuck up!" Micaela pushing her boyfriend away with ease. She grabbed Jaimi by the blouse and pulled her up.

Jaimi clawed her fingers across the face of her tormentor. She only had one fight in her life, a junior high brawl with Ruthie Franklin. What little she remembered about the experience was Ruthie clawing her thirteen-year-old nails down her face.

Now Jaimi scraped down with her own fingers.

"Bitch!" Micaela wailed in pain then pushed Jaimi back. The two women then grasped each others hands and arms, struggling to gain position. Untrained and unpredictable fighters.

Determined, Jaimi pivoted and pushed Micaela back.

The young woman fell backward into oncoming traffic.

A car honked.

A warning that came too late.

Tires screeched. The impact threw Micaela backward ten feet before she hit the ground, her body skidding across the asphalt.

Her skull cracked open like an egg, red yolk oozed out of the top of her head.

"They're not going to charge me," Jaimi said after Ian picked her up from the hospital. "Self-defense. Eyewitnesses corroborated that she attacked me first."

"Good."

Ian continued driving down the road in silence. He weaved through traffic, turned a corner and accelerated down an empty road.

"How do you feel?"

"Now that I've killed someone?"

Ian nodded.

"Looking forward to a good night's sleep," Jaimi said.

"It was an accident," Ian said with a hint of uncertainty. "You had to do what you had to do."

"I really wasn't going to go away with Timothy," Jaimi said. "And I didn't sleep with him. Just in case you were wondering."

"Okay," Ian said, his face turning tense.

"I was willing to do anything to save our son. Anything."

"I know."

"And now a woman is dead," Jaimi looked out the window and up at the sky as if addressing God. "I don't take that lightly. I hurt someone. Someone had to die so that our son can live. We know that."

"I think everything will be okay," Ian said. "Maybe-"

He stopped in mid-sentence as he looked into his rear-view mirror. A red Mustang pulled up behind him.

"No way," he whispered.

Turning her head around, Jaimi shuddered as she saw Dominic in the Mustang with Fiona.

The Mustang swerved around them and surged ahead.

"Go after them," Jaimi said, her voice hoarse with fear.

Ian hit the gas.

The faster he went, the more the Mustang accelerated.

Dominic hit a sharp right at the upcoming corner and Ian continued straight through a red light, losing them.

"Dammit!" she said. "Can't you drive!"

"Shut the hell up!" Ian said.

"You shut up! Can't you see they were turning!"

"Nothing changes," Ian said. "You always do that. Criticize! Criticize every little friggin' detail."

"Go back!" Jaimi said. "You're going to lose him."

His face red in anger, Ian made a U-turn and sped back down the street.

"Faster."

"I thought I told you to shut up," Ian hissed.

"Nothing changes," Jaimi said. "We're just like the way we were before. Just like our parents. And our parents before them."

Up ahead, they saw the red Mustang coming toward them at breakneck speed.

Ian slowed his car down. They could see the couple arguing in the car, replaying the scene from their dreams.

Jaimi reached over and tried to turn the steering wheel out of the way as the Mustang swerved into them. Both of their car horns blared.

Ian's car spun around then skidded to a halt.

"You alright?" he asked.

Jaimi sat frozen while she caught her breath.

Ian looked at the road in front of him and behind himself.

No Mustang in sight.

"It has to end," Jaimi said. "I have to end it."

"How?"

CHAPTER TEN

Ian listened to Jaimi's directions as she led them to the front of Timothy's apartment complex.

"Are you sure you don't want me to do it?" he asked, looking up at the dying vines growing up the side of the building.

"Don't act like you would be able to."

"I think I could."

"I know I can," Jaimi took out the gun from the dashboard.

"Might be better if I do it."

"I'll do it," she said. "I'll get less time in jail."

"I'm still an accomplice," Ian said, watching as Jaimi exited the car without another word and slipped the gun into her jacket.

She marched straight to Timothy's door, pounding on the wood. A chain could be heard becoming unhooked.

Timothy said nothing as he opened the door, his eyes bloodshot.

"I'm really sorry," Jaimi said.

Timothy nodded.

"Can I come in?"

He stepped aside and closed the door behind Jaimi.

"I didn't mean to lead you on the way I did."

"Is this a joke?" Timothy asked with a smirk on his face.

"What?"

"I meant to lead you on," Timothy shook his head. "You were my escape hatch. So I suppose I should thank you. Because you were right. I didn't want to marry Micaela. I didn't know how to escape. But now, thanks to you, my life just got a whole lot easier."

"Why?"

"I've been seeing her sister," Timothy said. "Iris. From the restaurant. It just happened. She's younger than Micaela. She has better personal qualities. We're having a baby."

"What?"

"She went to the doctor today. Two months pregnant. Doctors say it is going to be a girl."

"How did-"

"It was a one-time thing," Timothy said with a rotting smile. "We went out for a drink and we both lost our heads. But I always loved her. I just didn't realize it until I was about to go away with you. I wanted to run away. We didn't know how we were going to break it to Micaela and family. Now we don't have to. We can say we comforted each other during our loss. How cool is that?"

"Jesus," Jaimi whispered.

"We already have a name picked out," Timothy said. "Fiona."

Jaimi felt the earth die when she heard the name.

Ian reached over and held the door open for Jaimi as she exited the apartment.

His pulse quickened when he saw the ashen face of his ex-wife.

"What happened?"

"He has a little girl."

"What?"

"He got the sister pregnant."

"The sister?"

Jaimi nodded.

Ian watched as Jaimi gripped the pistol.

Looking up, they saw Iris walk up the steps to Timothy's apartment.

"Is that her?"

"Yeah."

"What is God trying to tell us?" Ian said. "We can't change the damn future. What is destined is destined."

The two remained silent for a beat. Jaimi stared down at the gun.

"We can't," Ian said. "We're not those kinds of people."

"I know that now."

"Me too."

The Mustang pulled up behind them. The sun beat down on the car, the glare not allowing Ian to see inside.

"When we got a divorce," Ian said. "I would just stare out the window. I used to see that red Mustang drive by. But I would never notice. I would just think about us."

"I would reach for you when I'd wake up," Jaimi said. "It was like a phantom pain."

"We should just go," Ian said. "We take Dominic and we pack our bags and we go. We drive and drive until we no longer see that damn car. We care about each other they way we should, with everything we have deep inside. We find out what we can really become. No more empty words. No more contracts of marriages and doing things just for people who don't really care about us anyway."

"We start new lives far away."

"We love each other," Ian said. "With everything we have."

Ian looked over at Jaimi. Taking a deep breath, he took her face in his hands and kissed her with as much tenderness as he could muster.

Then he put the car into drive and entered traffic.

The red Mustang followed.

"Nothing can pull us apart again."

"We can do this," Ian nodded. "For our son."

Jaimi leaned over and kissed him on the cheek. "For each other," she said, the words echoed as if released from a cage.

Ian put his arm around his wife. "Its time we dreamed of better things."

Looking into the rear-view mirror, he saw the red Mustang take a right turn.

And slip out of sight.

THE SCREAMS OF GHOSTS

57

ALEXIS RAYE

As she was about to close her email for the night and go to sleep, Sara heard that familiar little beep. A new message was waiting for her. It was an email sent through her YouTube account, which she had filtered as soon as her channel had taken off. It was only 9 months ago that she started uploading videos of her adventures but she had really started ghost hunting years earlier. As a kid, she and her brother would dare each other to go into the creepy abandoned houses on the other side of town. They fascinated her with their old architecture and their decrepit walls. She couldn't believe that houses that looked so lifeless, used to be alive with the sounds of families. Somehow, they never scared her, though she pretended to be for her brother.

She truly loved exploring them. What she loved even more was the attention she got from telling her friends about her brave trips inside. She never had enough of that. From the age of 8 and all the way through high school, she regaled anyone who would listen of dark stories filled with supernatural events that she made up off the cuff. Not everyone believed her but it was hard to deny how good of a story teller she was.

And as a new college graduate from a media arts school, she had dedicated her first year of adulthood into creating this persona of an extreme ghost hunter. Her success was overwhelming, even to her, and her fame seemed to grow exponentially every day. She was now even recognized on the street and asked for autographs. That, of course, made all of her sleepless nights and uncomfortable overnight stays in creepy old houses worth it.

The email was still bold as she clicked on it. It was an invitation to fly across the country to Louisiana sent from "The Conservation Collective of Pre-Civil War Phantasmal Plantations". She read it carefully.

Dear Ms. Sara Elliot,

The Conservation Collective of Pre-Civil War Phantasmal Plantations would like to extend an invitation for you and your crew to spend a night in one of our oldest and most spectral houses. It is called "The Lynch Plantation" named after its original owner, although its name holds appropriately with its history. Mr. Lynch was said to be the cruelest man in the south and lynched all of his slaves when he found out that the war had been won by the north. Surprisingly though, his story is not the one that the locals remember. Called Pi Beta Die by the locals, this house's last use was to house a sorority for the local university. 15 years ago, the maintenance man assigned to the house had a psychotic break and killed all 24 members of the sorority then hung himself on the porch outside.

It is our belief that the Lynch Plantation's history is enough to interest you but to further encourage you to create an episode for this house, we have arranged all of your travel and accommodations. You will see the details in the attached document.

The Conservation Collective of Pre-Civil War Phantasmal Plantations seeks to get more publicity and therefore more funding for our cause so please send your reply as soon as possible.

Best Wishes,

The CCPCWPP

She was hooked. Instead of going to bed as planned, she stayed up all night reading and researching the sordid history of the plantation. It was even more incredible, terrifying and mysterious than they had let on in the email. She knew that a night in this house would solidify her as YouTube's leading Ghost Hunter and may even lead to her getting her own show. She knew her fans well. They would love the creepy historical aspect and eat up the sorority massacre with a spoon. When she was too excited to wait, she dialed the number of her main camera tech Lila.

"Its 6:45am Sara, you better have actually seen a ghost," she grumbled. Lila wasn't a morning person and she had known Sara for long enough to know that most of her "ghost sightings" were fake and in fact was one of the people responsible for how real their "encounters" looked.

"Lila, if you wake up now and listen, I'll buy you Starbucks and give you a raise," Sara said. She knew Lila couldn't resist coffee.

"What is it?" she asked, sighing.

Sara beamed with enthusiasm. She knew that it was coming across through the phone because as she explained the email, Lila became more and more alert and excited.

"This could be huge for us Sara!"

"So you're in?" Sara said, knowing that she didn't even need to ask.

"Duh!"

"Ok ,we have to get the guys to agree too." Sara coached.

"Just promise them an adventure and to keep them when you get your own show," Lila said nonchalantly. Of course the rest of the crew would agree. The guys were in their mid-twenties and could be pacified with a cheeseburger.

The next few days were filled with preparation. Sara responded to the email to agree to the trip and outlined what she needed when they arrive and explained who she was bringing. The impression she got from the responses were that the more the merrier. Finally, they were all on a plane from Washington to Louisiana. The guys slept the whole way, snoring loudly of course. Sara and Lila sat together to write the script for the background and opening. They would shoot the outside of the plantation and house during the day and have shots of Sara explaining all the details she found about the mass lynching and murders.

By time they arrived, Sara and Lila had all of their shots planned and a script all laid out. Even though they were itching to go straight to the old house, The Conservation Collective of Pre-Civil War Phantasmal Plantations contact insisted they check into a hotel and get settled and rested. They would begin their investigation and shooting tomorrow. They were all smiles and splurged on room service and watched TV on the flat screen. The hotel was obviously very old but well-kept and the rooms were modernized for the guests' comfort. The lobby was small but elegant with two rows of white pillars that led out to the street. After they were stuffed, they decided they needed to walk it off by exploring the bustling town around them.

It was a warm October night so they skipped their jackets and made their way down the old fashioned road. The buildings were tall and thin and the antique street lights cast long shadows against them which no one else seemed to notice. The group weaved their way in and out of the busy streets watching the locals as they enjoyed the many bars and cafes. Andrew, one of the sound techs was mesmerized by the voodoo shops he saw and dragged Colin, another camera guy, in with him. He bought them all incense and they laughed as they all wandered the streets with the potent twigs. Finally they settled on a quiet smoky café. Knowing they had to be awake and alert the next day, they all opted for coffee or tea. As they sipped the delicious, hot beverages, they began to discuss the plan for the next day.

"Ok, I think we should be all packed by 11am. I want to make sure we can get to the location and have plenty of time to explore the plantation before sunset. We also need time to shoot the outside shots with the narrative and set up camp inside for the night," Sara said.

"I agree," Lila said. "Colin, I know you have that 4k camera that can work in low light. Hoorah for that. I was thinking we'll start outside and work our way in. We'll shoot like we always do, start in the living room, I'll explain the history of the house then we'll pretend we'll hear something and head upstairs."

"You want me to add a sound effect in post?" Colin asked.

"Yeah, of course," Lila said. "As long as its not too cheesy. Has to sound real. Like a ghost screaming or something."

"I have no idea what that would sound like," Colin laughed.

Lila covered her mouth and made a groaning sound. "Like that."

"Sounds like a bullfrog with indigestion."

Well, you know what I mean. We'll worry about all that later."

"Done deal."

"Of course, we will have to wait until we see it in person to make the final decisions but Sara and I have pretty much memorized the property maps and house floorplans." Lila finished.

"How creepy is it that it's called "Lynch"?" Andrew said.

Matt, their back-end video editor, chewed on some cookies as Andrew glanced his way.

"What? Just cuz I'm black you look at me?" Matt said jokingly. Andrew gave him a little, playful shove and they laughed.

"I'm just saying..." Andrew said with a laugh, "If there is some sort of evil ghost there... you might be the first to go."

Colin nudged Matt, "Don't worry man, I got your back!" Then they all started laughing.

Sara really enjoyed her crew. They were as silly as they were serious and worked as hard as she did. But they also brought her out of her head and gave her time to be sarcastic and have fun. She smiled at them. Then she saw a young woman lean over to Andrew.

"Excuse me... Uh... were you talking about going to the Lynch Plantation?" she asked, looking more than a little concerned.

Andrew grinned, apparently not picking up on her trepidation. "Yep! First thing tomorrow!"

The blood drained from her face. "Why... why would you go there?" she asked, her voice shaking.

"See that girl over there?" Andrew pointed to Sara. The girl nodded and Sara gave a little wave. "Well she is a ghost hunter and also a tiny dictator. We go where she tells us," he said sarcastically. A tone this young woman missed.

She looked directly at Sara. "You need to stay away from there."

Sara laughed nervously. "Oh come on... It's just a house. We will be there one night and that will be it."

The young woman looked even more terrified. "You're staying the night?!" she asked. Her voice carried enough that the rest of the people in the café turned to look at them. The soft music in the background stopped playing.

Sara and her team suddenly were the center of attention. Something that Sara was only comfortable with when it was filmed, not live. She looked at all the faces staring back at her. "Yea... that was part of the contract. My team and I have been paid to make a show for it... to raise money to restore it. It will bring more tourism to this town."

"Restore it?" the young woman asked. "We don't want it restored and we certainly don't want any tourists coming here only to be killed by going in that house."

The other patrons in the place nodded their heads in agreement.

"Listen, I have been all over the United States. I have stayed in over a hundred haunted houses. Nothing violent has ever happened and no one has ever been hurt." Sara said, choosing her words wisely. She wanted to tell them that all of this ghost business was crazy and that she had never encountered anything supernatural, but she didn't want that to get out and damage her show's credibility.

"All due respect... you've never stayed in this house." Another guy said from the corner. Sara's crew looked around at the petrified faces.

"So none of you ever go there? Even out of curiosity?" Colin asked.

"The last person that went there out of curiosity was found hanging from the porch the next day." The young woman replied.

"Maybe he was depressed and chose to off himself there." Andrew suggested while rolling his eyes. If anyone was a skeptic, it was him.

"He was my brother," she said. Andrew looked mortified and wished his tea had a shot of whiskey in it.

"Oops," he muttered, wishing he could say more.

"I'm sorry for your loss but we were paid to do something and we never back out of a contract." Sara said while Andrew stared at the table in front of him. "Now, I think we should be going." She said as they all stood up.

They shuffled out of the café and began walking towards the hotel quietly. They were all silently trying to brush off the many warnings they had just heard and get their excitement back.

"It's ok guys, some places just really buy into this crap." Lila offered.

"Yeah... but we have never had that reaction from any other location," Matt said. "Those folks are serious about this shit."

"Come on guys," Sara said. "This is a beautiful, creepy, historic building. It's going to be great, AND safe." They were probably just hazing the out of towners. I bet they're probably in there right now laughing their asses off at scaring us. Well, we'll let them think that way."

"Hey, uh... excuse me! Wait!" They heard someone say behind them. They turned. It was another young woman who had been listening silently in the café. She ran up to them and stopped. "Sorry, its just... we were wondering... who paid you to come here?"

"Um, it's a group called The Conservation Collective of Pre-Civil War Phantasmal Plantations. I believe they support and restore these kinds of places all over the south and have a lot in this area. I looked them up, their headquarters is just on the other side of town next to a Piggly Wiggly on 2nd street." Sara replied.

The girl looked around at the group with a strange expression. "That part of town has been completely abandoned for 10 years. There was a hurricane that destroyed it and we didn't have enough money to restore it... and as far as I know, there has never been a group by that name in this area. And I have lived her my whole life. I really don't think you should go to the plantation... someone is setting you up."

Sara looked uneasy but Andrew stepped forward.

"Listen, we appreciate your concern but I am sure there is a reasonable explanation. No one would spend this much money on a prank. Now tell all your buddies at the café that we aren't backing down."

Sara looked at the girl. If anyone had spoken to her like that she would have just let them walk straight into a moving car. But this girl stood there with panic on her face. She knew she couldn't say more but still looked like she wanted to stop them somehow. Her facial expression gave Sara goosebumps but before she could even consider breaking the contract, Andrew and Colin started leading her toward the hotel.

"This town is full of crazies." Matt said under his breath.

CHAPTER TWO

Sara didn't sleep well that night. The scene in the café played in her head over and over. She lay awake listening to everyone else snoring. Finally, she flopped over to look at the clock. It was 3:19 am. She groaned quietly. She thought about how excited she had been for this and managed to talk herself back into the adventure before her, deciding that the townies just didn't get out much and had possibly seen too many movies. She fell asleep.

By 11am exactly, their van was packed and any trace of hesitation from the night before was gone and the silliness had returned. Colin was shooting footage of their drive on his phone. Sara and Lila were taking selfies with all of the equipment. Andrew was driving, as always and Matt was snoozing in the front seat.

After a 40 minute drive, passing through the town, driving past the university, they finally pulled up to a large flat expanse. There was a dirt road jetting off to the left and a large sign above it that was covered in dust. Matt jumped out and managed to jump up to wipe the dust away. Sure enough it said "LYNCH". Colin couldn't help it, and he jumped out to take a picture of Matt standing under the sign with both hands flipping him off and a huge grin. They all giggled and rolled their eyes. Then they took off down the dusty dirt road. The large house grew as they neared it.

"I knew it was a mansion but I guess I didn't think it would be this big." Lila said.

"What do you think a sorority was thinking in buying something like this?" Sara asked.

"Simple, they could have keggers and ragers without the neighbors complaining." Colin said. He was the only one who had been a part of Greek life. A part of his past he tried to suppress.

They pulled up to the front of the house and climbed out. For a moment they just stood, appreciating its old fashion beauty and its size. It was gigantic. The wrap around porch alone was bigger than Sara's apartment. Sara and Matt continued to look over the house and the land while Lila, Colin and Andrew unpacked the equipment. When they finished, Lila walked up to Sara to make a game plan.

"It's hard to believe that the townspeople wouldn't want to save this place. It's so beautiful." Sara whispered.

"I know. Like look over there! Past that field it looks like there is a pond and small wooded area. And this tree over here would be great for a giant swing..." Lila said as she approached an old Oak tree that was closest to the house.

"Its really big. Like really big. This is going to be our best shoot yet," Sara said.

"Where should we start?" Lila asked.

Sara looked around thoughtfully. "Ummm... let's begin with the civil war history of the plantation and slaves with the fields in the background. Then I will walk to the tree and end at the porch when I talk about the sorority massacre. Got it?"

Lila nodded once and set up her camera. She began rolling as Sara started to talk.

"Hello, today we are in Louisiana at their best kept secret haunted destination. The Lynch Plantation is over 200 years old and has a most interesting history. Built by a Slave trader and his wife in the early 1800s, this plantation was one of the largest and most profitable in the area. Although aptly named for the fate of over 300 slaves, the Lynch plantation actually received its name from the slave trader who built it. James and Mary Lynch became exceedingly wealthy from the cotton cultivated here. Once the war was won by the north, they knew that their way of life would never be the same. Already know to be a cruel master, James Lynch decided that his final act of rebellion against the north was to kill all of the slaves he held. Most of them were hung from the branches of this oak tree but the younger children and smaller women were drown in the pond at the back of the property.

Then the bodies were collected, placed in a pile and burned at the entrance where you can still see bits of burn marks today. Only 5 years after the mass lynching, Mary Lynch suffered a psychotic break, claiming that the ghosts of those she helped kill were haunting her. She stabbed her husband and then hung herself on the porch right here. But perhaps the most famous suicide on this porch was that of mass murderer Gary Lindale. Gary, a maintenance man from the university was hired specifically to look after the needs of this house while it served as the Pi Theta Kai sorority house. He lived in a small servant house that used to stand just over there but has since been demolished. One night, Lindale snapped, much like Mary Lynch and went on a murdering spree killing every single sorority girl inside. He then called 911, left the phone off the hook and hung himself in the exact same place as Mary.

This house certainly is one of our more chilling explorations and we invite you to join us for a night at the Lynch Plantation." Sara said and stopped. That was the cue for Lila to stop rolling. It never ceased to amaze her that Sara could do these on the first take with no notes in front of her. She was a natural.

"Let's say we explore, take pictures and maybe some landscape footage?" Sara asked Lila and Colin.

Andrew and Matt were right behind, having a heated debate about which sorority girls they thought were the best partiers. Sara and Lila tuned them out, focusing on the expanse in front of them. The sun beat down and even in mid-October, the heat made them sweat. For a moment, Sara imagined what it would have been like to harvest in this heat as a slave. She let herself mourn the loss of the hundreds of innocent lives. She didn't believe in the afterlife so she hoped that death was a welcomed rest for them. They explored until the sun got low in the sky.

"Guys we should go inside and set up now." Matt said, turning to the house. They picked up the equipment from the ground outside and walked up the creaking steps to the front door. Lila pulled out a small camera and filmed Sara as she turned the doorknob and pushed. The door gave way with a small squeak. They slowly made their way inside. The entry way was covered in dust but other than that, it looked as though the owners had just stepped out for a moment. There was furniture set up as if company was expected. The long dining room table was set as though the sorority girls were going to sit down to dinner together. They made their way down the hall and through each room. Colin and Lila were shooting footage of everything. Finally they made their way to the living room. It was beautifully decorated and the fireplace even had logs in it ready to be lit.

"Matt and I will set up the cameras in the rooms and upstairs. Lila, you and Colin make sure that the feeds are working and tell us about positioning." Andrew ordered. He was excited. While the rest were busy with their tasks. Sara decided to watch the footage they had gotten before including her intro. She sat on the dusty old sofa and turned on the camera. The footage was even better than she had hoped and for a moment, she was extremely grateful that she had found such talent in Lila. As the video wrapped up she saw the frame of the entire house. Once more she took in the beauty until she noticed something. She paused the video and zoomed in. Up on the second floor in one of the bedroom windows stood a woman in a very old dress staring directly into the camera.

Sara took in a huge gasp of air and blinked. She looked again and the figure remained. She waved her hand toward Lila.

"What is it Sara?" She asked seeing Sara's horrified face.

"Colin, can you see me? How is this?" They heard from the microphone attached to the camera that Andrew was placing.

Lila moved over and looked at what Sara was pointing at. They replayed that part of the video and they were both speechless. They continued to watch through to the end and that was when they saw something even more startling. As Sara had approached the porch and was explaining Mary's hanging, the woman disappeared from the window and suddenly appeared right behind Sara holding a noose. They both gasped in fear.

"That's good Andrew, I think that's the best shot." Colin said into the walkie talkie.

Sara and Lila looked up to see the screen that Colin was watching. The video feed was of Andrew in the same room that the woman had been in in the video. "Andrew!" They both shrieked. Colin jumped in surprise.

"What?!" Andrew said from right behind them. They jumped and turned to him.

"How... you were just..." Sara stuttered.

"There is a 30 second delay. Geez what's wrong with you two?" He asked. They showed him the video while Colin helped Matt navigate setting up a camera in another room on the second story.

Andrew was just as stunned as they were. "I was just in there and there was nothing weird..." He said trying to talk himself down.

Then Lila got an idea. "Colin play back the footage you have of Andrew setting up the camera." She said.

"What..? Why?" He asked confused. He had been too distracted to hear their conversation.

"Just do it." Sara screeched. He did and they saw the room in night vision. It glowed in a soft green and they saw Andrew fumbling with the equipment.

"How long have you been doing this for now Andrew?" Colin teased but no one laughed.

Then just as Andrew leaned over to place the camera and backed away they saw her. The woman was right behind him holding a noose. Colin, who hadn't heard anything before that jumped back and screamed. "What the F***?!" They watched Andrew leave the room and the woman with the noose remained staring into the camera, unmoving. Then finally she turned her head and seemed to float out of the room.

They sat watching the camera in silence until the walkie talkie beeped, startling all of them.

"Colin, Colin! Is this ok? I don't want to be up here alone any longer. It gives me the creeps!" Matt said.

Colin immediately switched the video feed to Matt's camera only to see a close up of his face.

Sara held her breath. She wondered if the woman would appear in that room too. She grabbed the walkie talkie.

"Matt... uh... can you back up so we can see the room." She said with her voice shaking. They watched for 30 seconds and then saw him nod at the camera and back away. Just as they got a glimpse of the room, the feed cut and they heard a thud.

"Matt!" Sara screamed. They watched the screen and saw that it was flashing between black and night vison. When it stopped flashing, it showed something that drained Sara's blood. It was the woman holding the noose and standing next to a tall man in the same period clothing. And at the bottom of the screen they could see Matt's still body.

Andrew and Colin jumped up and ran to the staircase. Lila and Sara could hear their heavy footsteps above them. Lila stared at the screen with a strange expression on her face.

"Wait... that man... I've... I've seen him before. She reached for her laptop and opened it to a bookmarked page. It was an article from a newspaper covering the massacre of the sorority sisters. There were pictures of all 24 victims and a picture of the man who killed them. It was the same man.

Sara and Lila looked at both images in utter confusion. Then the feed from the room was cut completely and just as suddenly, the power went out. The darkness surrounded them and they screamed. In the corner of the room, a giant clock struck the hour. It was only 10 pm but it felt so much later. After the last chime, the power came back on and everything was quiet. Lila and Sara first checked to make sure the other was ok then looked around them. But when they looked at the walls, both felt as though the wind had been knocked out of them. All of the paintings, pictures and decorations were upside down.

They bolted up and ran to the stairway. As they climbed they saw the upside down portraits smiling sadistically at them. That's when Lila first saw it. Blood splatter on the wall. It looked fresh.

"Andrew! Colin! Matt!!??" She screamed and they ran up the stairs.

"Down here." Andrew's calm voice beckoned them to the last room on the right. Matt was sitting on the floor and Andrew was standing next to him. Colin was fiddling with the camera.

"I just told him what we saw." Andrew explained. "He doesn't believe me." Matt was clutching his head.

"What happened? Did they get you?" Sara asked breathlessly.

"Not you too... listen guys this isn't funny ok? My head hurts from knocking it on that shelf and I am not in the mood for a practical joke." Sara was about to try to reassure him that it was no joke when they heard the door behind them creak.

They turned to see a beautiful blond girl standing in the doorway. Her hair was disheveled and there was blood dripping from the side of her mouth and oozing from her sides and arms. "He's coming. You'd better run... although it never helped any of us." She said as her cold blue eyes looked past them to the window.

Then the lights went out again and flashed back on. She was gone and all that remained was a bloody hand print on the door frame.

"Believe me now?" Andrew said. Sara had no idea how he could care about that at a time like this.

"We need to leave." Sara said rushing to the door. But as she ran into the hall, she saw the same man as before wearing modern clothes and wielding a large knife. She saw blood splatter l lining the walls. He was blocking their way to the stairs. She looked around at the other bedroom doors that were slightly ajar. None of them would protect them. Then she looked up. There was a rope that pulled down a ladder to the attic.

"You guys!" She said as she yanked it. The man at the end of the hall started walking slowly towards her, undeterred by her possible escape. They all scrambled up the ladder and slammed the entry way shut before the man with the knife could reach them. They heard nothing. They sat in the dusty attic and silently tried to think of how to escape from the top floor of a mansion without going back into it. Though they were not really safer than before, the attic gave them a false sense of security and they all tried to breathe. Lila looked over at a box near them. She pulled out a very old painting. Though it was dark, she could make out that it was a couple. She pulled out her phone and used the light to look at the image. When she saw it clearly, she nearly dropped it.

It was the same man and woman they had seen in the video. But not only that, the man was identical to the mass murderer who killed the sorority girls 15 years prior. She read the bottom of the frame, "Mr. and Mrs. Lynch".

"Guys..." She said and showed the picture to the others.

"So what was this guy reincarnated or whatever?" Andrew asked. It was strange to hear that from a skeptic.

Just then, the ladder to the attic began to shake. They all looked around to find a way out. There was a tiny window at the other end of the attic. They ran over and Colin broke the old glass with his foot. Sara slid out first and they lowered her on to a part of the roof over the second story. Then it was Lila's turn. When they were both out, they crawled along the shingles to find a place they could climb down to the ground. They found nothing. By time the guys had slipped out, they had found the only possible way off the roof was to lower down into one of the bedroom windows. Andrew went first to break the window and help grab the others. Lila went first, then Colin. When it was Sara's turn she briefly looked around the property and the dirt road. The moon was much brighter than she thought it was and it lit the whole plantation. That was how she saw him. There standing against an old truck was a man, just watching the house and watching them climbing in. He didn't move.

"Do you see that man?" She asked Matt. He looked to where she was pointing and shivered. Something about the man by the truck gave him a sickening feeling.

"Yea... but we can't worry about him right now. We have to get out of here." Matt said.

He helped her lower down then quickly climbed down himself. They all made their way to the door and into the hall. Just as soon as they had stepped into the hall, the man reappeared with his bloody knife.

"Into the rooms!" Andrew screamed and they split up into each room.

They slammed the doors and turned the latches, each praying that the doors would hold from the phantom killer. But no sooner had they each locked the doors when a chorus of screams sounded. Hearing this, Sara turned around to face the room she was in. There was blood everywhere. The walls were covered and there on the bed was the body of a dead girl who had been stabbed over 10 times. Sara let out a cry. She heard the same sound come from Lila in the room next to her. They were all seeing the crime scenes of the girl that had died in each room.

Tears rolled down Sara's face. She ran to the window to try to open it. She would jump if she had to. A broken leg was better than dying. But it wouldn't budge.

"It won't open. They are nailed shut from the outside. He was very clever." A voice said from behind her. Sara turned to see the dead girl sitting up on her bed, the blood still dripping out of her wounds. He lifeless eyes seemed to look right through Sara. Sara screamed and rammed herself against the window. She would break the glass if she had to.

"You'll never make it. He planned this too well. The others that live here are loyal to him. They will help him to kill you. Just like they did for us." The dead girl said. Blood sprayed out of her mouth as she spoke but she didn't seem to notice. Sara tried not to look at her but felt a pulling sensation and her eyes were drawn back to the blood soaked girl on the bed. As soon as she made eye contact the lights went out again then flashed back on. The room was clean and the girl was gone. Then the door swung open. But the hall was empty. Sara poked her head out just enough to see her crew doing the same. They bolted towards the stairs only to see 24 bloody girls standing at the bottom staring up at them.

"He likes the chase. He likes the chase." They all chanted in a haunting harmony. Then they began climbing the stairs. They turned back to the hallway to see the man with the blade and the woman with the noose.

They moved towards them, slowly at first but then began to speed up, disappearing and reappearing closer and closer. Colin panicked and ran into the closest bedroom and slammed the door. Sara could him them trying to break the window. The woman with the noose smiled as she walked right through the door. There was a crashing sound then a thud. Then the door swung open slowly. Lila ran in to see if Colin had made it but as soon as she peered out the window she let out a horrible scream. She saw Colin swinging below from a noose. She turned back to look at her friends in horror but the door slammed shut once more and both phantoms were gone.

Seconds later there were terrible screams and then a gurgling sound. And once more the door swung open slowly. Lila was on the bed covered in her own blood with stab marks all over her body. Her eyes were looking up to the ceiling as if looking a God.

Sara almost ran into her but Matt grabbed her. He turned to look at the mob of dead sorority girls who stood staring with vacant expressions repeating, "He likes the chase."

"Help us!" He screamed. They ignored him. He grabbed Sara's arm and pulled her into the crowd.

"They aren't going to hurt us. They are his victims." He said and he and Sara ran down the stairs. Andrew couldn't move, he was frozen in fear. Andrew had never believed in the supernatural and couldn't process it. Matt and Sara ran to the front door and flung it open. Sara was about to yell for Andrew but at that very moment they saw a body drop from above the porch and swing in the same spot that Mary Lynch and Gary Lindale had hung themselves year before.

"Andrew!!!" Sara screamed. Matt dragged her to the car and fumbled with the keys. Finally he opened the doors and they both got inside and locked the doors. Sara looked at the house, now able to see it clearly in the moonlight. She saw Andrew's and Colin's bodies hanging from their nooses and looked up to the bedroom where Lila had been murdered. In the window stood the man with the knife. Next to him, stood a lifeless Lila. In all of the other windows, the Sorority sisters stood looking out into the night with their dead stares. Matt revved the engine and turned the van sharply to get back on the dirt road. That's when they saw the man with the truck. He stared at them. His gaze was unwavering. After a few moments he got in his truck and turned on his bright lights. Then he revved his engine and slammed on the accelerator. He was driving right at them.

"What the F*** is he doing?" Matt asked in shock. He didn't have time or room to get out of the way and Sara braced herself for the impact. But as soon as the truck would have touched the front fender, it disappeared. Matt looked around and in the rear view mirror. There was no sign of it.

"Just go!" Sara yelled.

And they did. They drove to the police station and told them everything that had happened. The police refused to go to the house until the morning and Matt and Sara stayed in their cell the rest of the night.

In the morning they all went back. It was just as they had left it. The police did their reports and the coroner was called. When they had gotten all their equipment out, Sara asked if they could leave. One of the cops agreed to take them back to their hotel and they climbed in the back of a car. Sara let her look once more at the big house. She looked up at the room where Lila had died. There in the window was Lila looking back at her. She waved a sad goodbye and disappeared.

Sara was institutionalized a week later and this is the only story she will ever tell.